I was thrilled to receive "The Shadow in the Chasm" authored by Joyna Sehgal, a young student at St. Xavier's Sr. Sec. School, Chandigarh. The story is a masterful blend of fantasy with liberal dashes of humour and generous pinches of wit, bound together with freshness and intensity. This fun, quick-paced story will not disappoint the reader. This is Joyna's first attempt in the literary field. Bravo!

– Dr. Ivorine Castellas
Principal
St. Xavier's Sr. Sec. School, Chandigarh

It was exhilarating to read this. Couldn't believe myself. You are an inspiration to many including me. Best wishes for a great life full of joy and books and reading and writing.

– Ravi Santhanam
Chief Marketing Officer
Head – Corporate Communications, Liability Products & Managed Programs at HDFC Bank

Such a great piece by a young writer. No words. Just applause.

– Nishant
Writer & Editor, Times of India, Chandigarh

This book will take you into another world. The author has imbued this book with humour, charm and cleverness that will both amuse and delight children and adults. This book is highly recommended to all those who love magic, wizards, thrill and action. Best wishes to the budding author for her future endeavours.

– Deepika Arya
Senior English Teacher
St. Xavier's Sr. Sec. School, Chandigarh

Title – The Shadow in the Chasm

Author – Joyna Sehgal
ISBN – 978-93-92210-01-3
Edition – I

Published by –
J.G.S. Enterprises Pvt. Ltd.
(Imprint: The Browser)

Publisher's Address –
SCO 14-15, Sector 8-C, Chandigarh 160009

Website – www.thebrowser.org
Email – service@thebrowser.org

Printed in India

THE BROWSER

THE SHADOW IN THE CHASM

Joyna Sehgal

THE BROWSER
Publishers and Booksellers
www.thebrowser.org

Acknowledgements

My heartfelt gratitude to the Almighty for His grace and love.

A loving thanks to my parents and grandparents for their unconditional love and support, for guiding me on my journey, and for believing in the unbelievable.

Huge gratitude to my foundation – my school, our worthy principal and teachers who have always encouraged me and felt great about my achievements. A special thanks to my mentor, Japleen Kaur, for bringing out the best in me.

I would also like to acknowledge the support of my friends and well-wishers, and lots of good wishes to my readers for their time and love.

Joyna Sehgal

About the Author:

*Joyna is a budding author and
a great admirer of J.K. Rowling.
She believes in a world beyond
imagination and will take you on a
ride which keeps you engaged
through a mysterious storyline.*

CONTENTS

CHARACTERS

Fiona

A sharp tomboy with brown, blunt hair, long legs, and grey eyes, Fiona loves adventures. She is an orphan and the sister of Clemence.

Clemence

An intelligent girl with long and blond hair, long legs, and blue eyes, Clemence is an orphan too and Fiona's sister.

Zyrian

The man who is the cause of all the trouble in LOGSTON, Zyrian's appearance is scary – shoulder-length hair, a face with cold-blooded black eyes, half-covered with a black mask.

Chapter 1

Manell – The Dome 10/09/2020

(Manell – The main dome in the middle of the city)

Zyrian *(arrogantly)*

Yes! Now this place is mine. I won't let any stupid girl kill me.

(Laughs loudly.)

Glinda *(a young lady with confidence)*

You won't be able to succeed in it and I am telling you this.

Zyrian *(with a hint of fear and passionate desire)*

Of course! I will, after I kill you.

'Syldona!' *(Zyrian throws a killing spell on Glinda.)*

(Glinda casts a protective charm around her but the curse pierces right through it.)

(Glinda screams and dies.)

(Outside a young lady in her twenties is holding two babies – both of them crying – when she hears Glinda scream. A man standing in front of her tells her to run and take them away. She refuses, sobbing all the while. The man tells her that he will explain what has happened, but for now, she should take the children and leave. She doesn't want to, but deep down, she knows he is right. So, she finally concedes and after one last look she takes the babies and goes far away from there.)

Chapter 2

The Black Circular Spell - 10/09/2035

Fiona *(to Clemence, in their academic class)*

This is so boring! I want to leave this class right now. I need some adventure in my life.

Clemence *(to Fiona)*

Adventures! Weird.

(Suddenly the electricity goes off.)

Fiona

Yes! Finally, I do not have to listen to this boring lecture anymore.

Clemence

Yeah but...

(Unexpectedly, the girls feel something unusual.)

Fiona

Wait! Do you feel strange?

Clemence

Yea...

Fiona

What's happening? This is getting weird, don't you think?

(Clemence nods.)

Miss Kate (*their teacher*)

Kids, the power supply will resume in a few minutes. Don't worry.

Fiona

Ahh! This is getting into my nerves now.

(The lights are back.)

Clemence

It's stopped now! What just happened?

Fiona

No idea!

Miss Kate

Kids, the class time is over. You may leave.

(All kids start to leave.)

Clemence *(on their way out)*
Phew! That is over.

(Outside the class, the black circular spell starts to circle the girls again but nobody else can see it except them.)

Clemence
Now, what's this?

Fiona
Umm! I don't know.

(The girls start to move their hands here and there in the air to get rid of it.)

Ron (a boy sitting near them)
Have you girls lost your mind? What are you doing?

James (a boy sitting near Ron)
I think they have really lost it.

(Both boys laugh together.)

Clemence

Huh! Why?

Ron *(laughing)*

'Cause you're both swinging your hands crazily.

Fiona

Can't you see this black fog around us?

James

Of course not! There is nothing around you!

(The black spell vanishes and the girls exit in a weird mood.)

Clemence

This is getting...

(Fiona interrupts her and starts to talk.)

Fiona

Yeah, I know you are going to say 'odd' and it really is getting quite odd.

(The girls reach their house and go to their separate rooms.)

Chapter 3

The Letter

(Inside Fiona's room, the black spell surrounds Fiona again.)

Fiona

Ah! Not this again.

(The black spell drops a letter and Fiona then calls Clemence)

Fiona *(shouting at top of her voice)*

Clemence! Clemence!

(Fiona heads to Clemence's room and sees her sleeping.)

Fiona *(sarcastically)*

GOOD MORNING, CLEMENCE!

Clemence

H-huh? W-what?

Fiona

You're finally awake! I shook you, tickled you, even slapped you lightly but you still did not get up. So, I yelled straight into your ear. Clever, right?

Clemence *(sleepily)*

Sure... so, what brought you here?

(Still yawning!)

Fiona

Okay, now listen carefully. When I went to my room, the black fog surrounded me again and dropped a letter.

Clemence

What! Which letter? Okay, show me the letter.

Fiona

I will if you will let me.

Clemence *(being her nerdy self)*

Show fast! Time waits for no one!

(Fiona hands the letter to Clemence who looks shocked

upon opening it. Fiona sees her shocked face and quickly glances through the letter.)

Fiona

What! There is nothing in it.

Clemence

No, it can't be.

Fiona

Well, it is!

Clemence

Wait, do you see that?

Fiona

See what?

(There is something written on it but no one can read it. An irritated Fiona crumples the letter and throws it in the fireplace. Suddenly, the blood red ink begins to form words on the scroll.)

Clemence *(picking the letter in haste)*

Look at that... it says

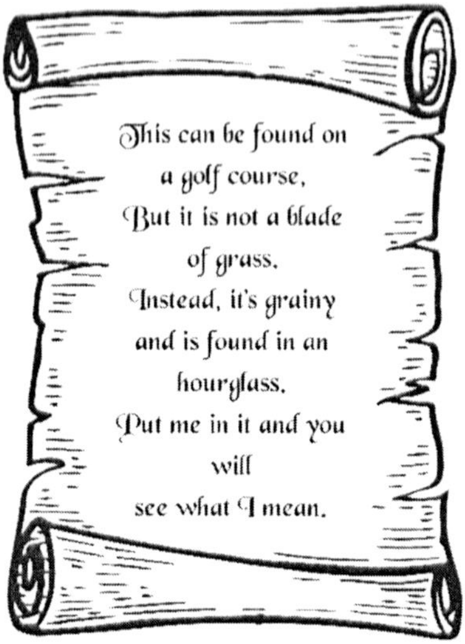

Fiona

What is that? What is present in the golf course but it's not grass, it is grainy and present in an hourglass? This is confusing!

Clemence

No, it's not if you solve the puzzle correctly.

Fiona

Yeah! But what is it?

Clemence *(speaking and thinking simultaneously)*

Umm, it is in a golf course but is not grass, it is

grainy and present in an hourglass. (*She thinks for a while.*) I think it is sand.

Fiona

Yeah, it's sand. It matches perfectly. It is present in a golf course, it is grainy, and is present in an hourglass. But why will someone put a letter in the sand?

Clemence

Let's just try. You don't know what can happen unless you try. Nobody saw the black fog either – only we [illegible] saw it. And, of course, instead of getting burnt, the [illegible] became readable when it was thrown in the fire. How [illegible] that even possible?!

Fiona

Okay, I get it. Let's go to the backyard.

Chapter 4

The Quest and the Dream

(As they start to gather some sand their caretaker enters.)

Cordelia *(the caretaker)*
Girls, what are you doing?

(The girls quickly hide the letter behind them.)

Clemence *(nervously)*
N-nothing! W-we are doing nothing.

Cordelia *(suspiciously)*
Umm, but what's a pile of sand doing there?

(Fiona and Clemence get scared but Cordelia remains determined to get an answer.)

Fiona
We are working on a project.

(The backyard fills with silence for a few moments.)

Cordelia *(says to herself)*

It can't be a project. Is it a letter from Lord Bavmorda? If it is, then the girls must know the truth.

(Cordelia exits the yard without saying a single word, leaving the girls alone.)

Fiona

She is gone now. Let's do it, come on.

(They both nod at each other and dip the letter in the sand pile. The letter sinks in it and after a while, it appears again with some words written on it.)

Fiona

Look it says... *(while reading the letter)*

Wow, so now we are superheroes! But what's LOGSTON, and who wants to destroy the world?

Clemence *(in confusion, pointing to a line in the letter)*
You just looked at that, but see it also says:
______ *You have been chosen!*

Fiona
This is getting messier.

(Fiona waits for Clemence's reply but gets none. She turns towards Clemence and sees her lying down on the ground. Clemence keeps mumbling something like 'this place must be old...' Fiona tries to wake her up but nothing works.)

(Clemence is in a trance. She sees a tomb and thinks aloud, 'It must be a very old place. Even the tomb looks like no one has ever kept a foot in it'. Her thoughts are interrupted by someone. She turns around and sees a young lady holding two babies and another woman saying to her, 'Get the girls away from here. Get them away from LOGSTON! They are not safe here.')

Fiona

Clemence! Are you okay? What happened to you?

Clemence

Yeah, I am okay but I saw a dream in which someone was holding two babies and a woman was shouting to take them away...
(Fiona interrupts her.)

Fiona

Away?! Away from where?

Clemence *(recalling the dream)*

LOGSTON! That person said LOGSTON. But why? This is getting more and more complicated. I think we need to go to LOGSTON.

Fiona

WHAT! HAVE YOU GONE CRAZY? How are we going to go there? We do not even know where it is.

(But somewhere in her heart, Fiona knows that they will be going there very soon.)

Clemence

Yeah, I know, but if we go there, only then will we be able to sort this out. To know, where this place is, we need to check the map of Italy.

Fiona

How do you know it's in Italy?

Clemence

Because the dome I saw behind the lady holding the babies is in Italy and I think we have seen it before. So, LOGSTON must be in Italy… One more thing, I think the babies I saw were you and me because I have seen you when you were young and one of the babies looked just like you.

Fiona *(in a sarcastic tone)*

Okay, so you mean to say, we both were in your illusion thingy. *(She adds air quotes with it.)*

Clemence *(with a little smirk on her face)*

Yup! I am shocked you got that on your first try.

Fiona

Ugh! You know what, leave it and open the map of Italy.

Clemence

I am not sure what to say. Are you agreeing with me? Did the sun rise from the west today?

Fiona

Oh, shut up!

Chapter 5

Finding LOGSTON

(Fiona takes out her laptop from a bag and opens the map of Italy)

Fiona

Well, this is it, we need to look for LOGSTON now.

Clemence

Umm, let's start from the top.

Fiona

Wait, you said that the woman in your dream was shouting, 'Take them away from LOGSTON.' Then it surely means it's away from where we live now because we were taken away from it. Since we live in the north now, LOGSTON is surely not at the top of the map.

Clemence

Right! So, let's look at the south first.

(They both start searching the map but are unable to find anything.)

Fiona

Where is this LOGSTON?!

Clemence

How on earth should I know?! It's in Italy because I saw that, but there's no place with this name on the map.

Fiona

Where should we hunt for it then? *(Thinks quietly for a while.)* Wait, remember, you said someone was holding us? What if it is Cordelia! She will know where LOGSTON is!

Clemence

Yeah, but I don't think she will tell us.

Fiona

Maybe, but it's worth a try! Come on!

Clemence

Fine!

Chapter 6

The Magical Hailet

(Clemence and Fiona enter the kitchen.)

Fiona *(to Cordelia)*
We want to ask you something.

Cordelia *(as if she knew this would come)*
Go ahead, ask.

Clemence
So, the first one is...

(Cordelia interrupts her)

Cordelia
There is more than one?

Fiona
Yeah!

Cordelia
Okay, so what's the first one?

Clemence

Where is LOGSTON?

Cordelia *(with a slight fear in her voice)*

What is LOGSTON?

Fiona *(curiously)*

Well, you know what it is. So, please open up. It is important for us to know!

Cordelia *(with lack of confidence)*

Look, I don't know what you are talking about.

Clemence

You know exactly what we are talking about!

Cordelia

I might say I do know where it is, but what are both of you up to now?

Fiona

So, you lied! You do know where LOGSTON is. You must take us there immediately and only then will we tell you everything.

Cordelia

You have to first tell me what you are up to.

Fiona

Nope.

Cordelia

Listen, only after hearing what is happening, I will decide if, and how, I can take you both there.

Clemence

What do you mean by 'decide'? We will go there by car or plane, right?

Cordelia *(laughing at their innocence)*

No! We can't go to LOGSTON like that.

Fiona *(through gritted teeth)*

Okay, fine I'll tell you.

Cordelia *(smirking)*

You have no choice.

(Fiona and Clemence tell her everything and Cordelia listens in complete silence.)

Cordelia *(astonished)*

So, did all this happen – black fog, letter, dream?

Fiona

Yup!

Cordelia

Okay, let's not waste any more time and let's get going.

Fiona

Wait, so you are taking us? I thought you wouldn't believe us!

Cordelia

Well, why wouldn't I? After all, I am a witch.

(The girls are shocked. There is silence. Clemence breaks it after a long pause.)

Clemence

WHAT! So, you are telling us magic is real?

Cordelia

Of course! I thought you might have believed it by now.

Clemence

Uh, well it's kind of difficult to believe in it.

Fiona

Let us leave all that for later. For now, shall we proceed to LOGSTON as we have a mystery to solve. Remember?

Cordelia

Oh yes! Let's go. (*Cordelia takes them to their backyard.*)

Clemence

What are we doing in the backyard?

Cordelia

Oh! Well, we are going to LOGSTON.

Fiona (*stunned*)

From the backyard?

Cordelia

You see, someone said, 'The greatest secrets are always hidden in the most unlikely places.'

Clemence

True!

Fiona

Never heard of that but, if you say so. Right now, I am just curious to know about how we are going to reach LOGSTON.

Cordelia

Oh yes! *(reciting)*

> It is such a secret place, the land tears,
> and those who don't believe in magic will
> never find it, I solemnly swear.

(A little pond appears in the ground of the yard.)

Fiona

What's a pond doing in our backyard?

Cordelia

Oh! It's not a pond, it's a Hailet.

Clemence

And what is that?

Cordelia

Hailet is like a pond that allows witches and wizards to connect with LOGSTON and WIZODRELL.

Clemence

Can you explain in brief what LOGSTON is?

Fiona

You sound like you are asking her a definition of a town in a city.

Cordelia *(sarcastically)*

Ha-ha, very funny.

Fiona

I know right.

Clemence

Cordelia, ignore her. You please continue to explain.

Cordelia

Hmm! So, LOGSTON is like a town where witches and wizards from all over the world come to buy and sell magical stuff. Some even live there.

Clemence

And explain WIZODRELL too.

Cordelia

Okay, so WIZODRELL is a school where young witches and wizards come to learn magic. Students who study there are called Wizodrellies.

Fiona

Interesting! So, shall we go to LOGSTON now?

Cordelia

Yes, we shall.

Clemence

But how?

Cordelia

At the bottom of this pond, there are two doors and you need to follow me through one of the doors. Remember, you don't need to hold your breath, you can breathe in Hailet's water. Understood?

Fiona and Clemence together

Yup!

Cordelia

Good. Let's go!

(All three of them dive into the pond. Surprisingly, it is very deep and everything is dark. Suddenly, the girls see a ray of light coming from Cordelia's side. She leads them to the bottom of Hailet and they see a door with LOGSTON written on it. They all go through that door and find solid ground beneath them. After a few seconds, a small stout woman appears in front of them.)

The Stout woman *(speaking in a squeaky voice)*

Welcome to LOGSTON.

Cordelia

Girls, meet Atom Bitsy, also known as Amelia Bitsy.

Amelia Bitsy

Hi, Cordelia! I am seeing you after a long time. And who are these cute girls?

Cordelia

They are Glinda's daughters, Atom.

Amelia Bitsy *(Beads of sweat on her forehead)*
G-Glinda's daughters?!

Cordelia
There is no need to worry, Atom.

Amelia Bitsy
O-Okay...C'mon all of you.

Clemence
Where are we going, Cordelia?

Cordelia *(with a smile)*
We are entering LOGSTON.

L — Townlet of houses
O — Chasm
G — Market
S — Lizoria
T — Castle
O — Blood Lake
N — Forest

Chapter 7

The Lord Bavmorda

Amelia Bitsy *(taking them to a door)*
There you go, Cordelia.

Cordelia
Thank you, Atom.

Amelia Bitsy
It's alright.

Fiona
Okay, so shall we go?

Cordelia
Oh yes, of course!

Amelia Bitsy
Bye girls!

Clemence
Bye!

Cordelia *(after not hearing a reply from Fiona)*
Fiona?

Fiona
Sorry, I didn't mean to drift away. I was thinking and yes, thank you Atom. Hope to see you soon.

Cordelia
Bye, Atom!

Amelia Bitsy
Now, I will get going.

(Amelia heads back to the first gate.)

Cordelia *(looking concerned)*
What were you thinking about?

Fiona
Oh, just about why Atom Bitsy was scared of us?

Cordelia
She is not scared of you. She was just emotionally attached to Glinda which is why after hearing her name after a long time, she got emotional. Those are enough questions for now. Let's go.

(Cordelia, Clemence, and Fiona go through the door. As Cordelia closes the door behind her and turns back to the girls, she sees their jaws dropping wide and their faces in shock.)

Cordelia

Are you both okay?

Fiona *(a bit shocked)*

Yeah, I just wanted to make sure if you are seeing what we are seeing. I mean, how come we are at this huuuge height?

(Cordelia had forgotten to tell them that they were going to be at about half the height of Mt Everest.)

Cordelia

Oh, girls, I forgot to tell you that this is the tower of LOGSTON, and it is quite high. The words you see down there, I mean, the land framed as letters of the word L-O-G-S-T-O-N, well, that's LOGSTON.

Fiona

Quite high? 'Quite' would be an understatement to describe this height.

Clemence *(nodding in agreement)*

How do we get down there and what do we have to do there?

Cordelia

We will use Hailet's water and we will do what we have to once we are there.

Fiona

Cordelia, we are humans, not fishes! We can't use water and what is the point of using water?

Cordelia

Fiona, what's the problem with water? Don't forget water is essential, especially in LOGSTON. Most things here can be done by using water.

Clemence

Listen, you have to tell us some rules before we go. I mean I don't want to look stupid in front of anyone. You see it's awkward.

Cordelia

I get it, but not now. We don't have time. Come on, follow me.

Clemence

Bu…

(Fiona interrupts her)

Fiona *(mimicking Cordelia)*

No ifs, no buts, follow Cordelia.

Cordelia *(sarcastically)*

Thank you, Fiona, but we got to hurry.

(Cordelia takes them to a bottle which is floating in the air, takes out three drops, and places them on each one's palm. She whispers a chant and then tells the girls to drink it. They do as she says. Suddenly, all three of them vanish. The girls feel like they can't breathe. But it stops soon enough, and they are all at the bottom of the tower. They exit the tower and Cordelia takes them between two hills on the T of LOGSTON. She tells the girls that she has to go back and that they should wait there till a man in a white robe appears. The girls start to question her but she ignores them and walks away.)

Fiona

Now, what do we do?

(The man, as mentioned by Cordelia, appears between the two hills in his white robes.)

The Strange Man

I'll tell you... I am Bavmorda. I have called you here because this place is special. It has a story, a story that relates to you and a story that has never been forgotten. No questions for now.

Fiona *(whispering sarcastically)*

Rule number 1 of LOGSTON – no questions.

Lord Bavmorda

I heard that.

(Clemence giggles.)

Lord Bavmorda *(handing them two sticks)*

Here you go, girls!

Fiona

What are these sticks? What do we do with them?

Lord Bavmorda

These are wands, I hope you girls know what a wand is?

(The girls nod and Lord Bavmorda continues)

Lord Bavmorda

There are many spells in this world but the most powerful one is Unioft, and to destroy the one who wants to take over the world, you need to use Unioft. Unioft is designed for both of you. I will teach you some spells but I can't teach you Unioft – you have to figure it out on your own.

Clemence

Why can't you teach us Unioft?

Lord Bavmorda

The spell is made for you and only for you two to find out.

Fiona

Okay, so we are ready! You can start teaching us from today.

Lord Bavmorda

No, from tomorrow, because it is getting dark, and the dark is the time for Earl Zyrian.

Fiona

Who is he? And why are you calling him Earl?

Lord Bavmorda

Earl Zyrian is second to none. He is the one and the only person who had the guts to go against your father. He is the one with whom you are going to fight. We call him Earl because he is one of those who know the full *Charten* of atrocious memories, black magic, and even dark curses.

Clemence

What! What is a *Charten*?

Lord Bavmorda

The Charten is a book that has dark instruments, magic and dreadful memories. Not everyone is allowed to read it. Earl Zyrian was not allowed to read it, but he broke the rules of Lord Abraham and read it. The reason why *The Charten* cannot be read by everyone is that it contains magic beyond what a normal wizard can ever imagine. As Earl Zyrian read *The Charten* without permission of the Superior, he had to face the repercussions for the same. Before you start asking about the Superior, let me tell you, he is a person who is the head of the whole magical world and your father,

Abraham, was 'The Superior' at the time when Zyrian read the book. Going back to where I was – if a person reads *The Charten* without the Superior's permission, he gets a curse for a lifetime, a curse that will make him weaker as he ages.

Fiona

What happened to our parents and Earl Zyrian?

Bavmorda

Girls, enough for now. I will tell you the rest later.

Clemence

Please tell us what happened to our parents.

Bavmorda

No, I can't. *(Bavmorda points towards a castle.)* You girls need to sleep there. Tomorrow we will start with the practice.

Clemence

What practice?

Fiona *(mockingly)*

Remember rule number 1 – no questions! *(everybody chuckles.)*

Chapter 8

Unioft – The Ultimate Spell

(The girls are lying on a bed.)

Fiona

Hey! Aren't you confused about everything that is happening? We were normal girls till yesterday and are witches now with magical powers –unbelievable, right?

Clemence

Yeah! But I am more worried about what happened to our parents.

Fiona

Yes, that indeed is a big mystery. I am sure we will get to the bottom of it. But for now, I guess we should go to sleep. I predict a big day for us tomorrow.

Clemence

Yeah! We should.

(Both girls try to sleep but they can't. They are trying

to figure out what the matter is. Ultimately, they decide to ask Lord Bavmorda about it the next day. The next day, between the hills, the girls are ready to ask but Lord Bavmorda does not let them ask anything, and instead, tells them that they will know everything after they defeat Earl Zyrian.)

Lord Bavmorda *(keeping the focus on teaching the spells)*
The first spell we are going to learn is the 'copy' spell. With this spell, you can copy anyone's face or voice. This will help you in defeating The Great Earl.

Clemence
Okay, but how do we use it?

Lord Bavmorda
For that, you girls need to take out your wands, say
'Mimicus'
and imagine who you want to become. But always remember one thing – your arm should be straight when you are casting your spell. You should feel the power of magic running through your veins.

Fiona
Wow, that's cool!

Clemence

I know, right!
(The girls learn several other spells like this.)

Lord Bavmorda

Girls, it's time for you to sleep now as you need to wake up early tomorrow.

Fiona

Yeah! I am feeling sleepy too.

Clemence

Okay, as you say.

Lord Bavmorda

Girls, I wanted to tell you that as I have taught you the main spells, you can go and explore LOGSTON in the morning.

Fiona

Yeah! That's a good idea.

Clemence

So, can we sleep now?

Lord Bavmorda

Certainly.

(The girls go towards the castle to sleep. Once asleep, they have a dream.)

A Strange Woman

Hi, girls hope you remember me. I just want to tell you that when the time will come and you will fight against Earl Zyrian, it will be a very difficult fight and you are yet to figure out Unioft, the most powerful spell. Bavmorda has also given you time to figure out, but if you can't figure it out on your own, then I can help. There is a stone buried deep in LOGSTON. It has the colour cyan and is mighty powerful. No one, other than me and your grandmother has ever seen it. However, the stone is way more powerful than Earl Zyrian. When the stone is used on him, he will dissolve to death. That's all that I had to say. I thought this information might help you. I need to go now, but you girls need to save the world. I came here to tell you this. God bless you, girls.

Clemence

Mom! Wait!

Chapter 9

The Brave Glinda in the Dream

(Both the girls wake up and realise that they had the same dream.)

Fiona *(after hearing Clemence say 'Mom')*
Hey! What was that?

Clemence
I don't know.

Fiona
I also had mom in my dream; she said we would need the help of the stone to defeat Earl Zyrian.

Clemence
But we can also figure out Unioft.

Fiona
It will take years for us to figure that out!

Clemence
You think so? Let us find the stone then. But I don't want you to doubt your ability. Know that

you are much more powerful than you think you are.

Fiona

You think so?

Clemence

Yes, I do.

Fiona

How do we find the stone?

Clemence

By digging to the bottom of every clue that comes our way and believing in ourselves. The most powerful magic is believing in oneself.

Fiona *(grinning)*

Okay, Miss Scholar, tomorrow we will go and look for that stone.

Clemence

Yeah! Let's get ready to save the world.

Chapter 10

Exploration Gone Wrong

(Lord Bavmorda tells the girls to explore and the girls start from the L of **L***OGSTON – a townlet of houses. They go further and reach the O of L***O***GSTON and see a chasm. The girls go to the bottom of the chasm, using Hailet's water, and see an oval-shaped portal made from Acasta Gneiss, the oldest-known intact crystal fragment on earth. There's a uniquely shaped button on the portal. Both get curious, so they press the button. Shortly after, Lord Bavmorda appears.)*

Lord Bavmorda

Girls, what are you doing here?

Fiona

We were just exploring and found this place! What is this?

Clemence

Yeah, please tell us!

Lord Bavmorda

I will, but first, we need to get away from here; this

place is dangerous.

Clemence

Umm, sure.

(The girls and Lord Bavmorda go towards the L of LOGSTON.)

Fiona

Now tell us what it was!

Lord Bavmorda

Girls that was a Portal through which Earl Zyrian and his followers can come to LOGSTON.

Clemence *(anxiously)*

Oh, but Bavmorda, we saw a button on the side of the Portal. What does that button do?

Fiona

Yeah! That button had a pretty intriguing shape and looked quite old. I am not even sure if it works.

Lord Bavmorda

Oh my God! I hope you guys have not pressed that button.

Clemence

What if we did press it? I don't think it will make any difference.

Lord Bavmorda *(knowing that the portal is now open)*

It will make a difference! That button turns the Portal on. Now, Earl Zyrian can enter LOGSTON any time. We MUST turn it off, girls.

Fiona

But it's already been 15 minutes, Bavmorda.

Lord Bavmorda

Oh no! This is not okay. He can enter anytime now and it's really dangerous to go near the Portal.

Clemence *(with fear)*

What shall we do now?

Lord Bavmorda

We must prepare to fight... fight hard ...and fight to win.

Chapter 11

The First Fight

(Near the hills, on the T of LOGSTON, the girls are thinking how to switch off the Portal while from behind a female follower of Earl Zyrian appears.)

Blink *(her voice dripping with venom)*

Well, well! Look who is here! Bavmorda, long time no see and who are these little girls?

Lord Bavmorda

Girls quickly go between the hills!

(The girls start to run but Blink is way faster than them. She blinks her eyes and reaches in front of the girls; they start to run back towards Bavmorda and hide behind him.)

Lord Bavmorda

Blink, leave them alone. They are just kids.

Blink

But I guess, they know everything – who they are and why they are here, who Earl Zyrian is and how they are connected. I am pretty sure that they even know what happened in the past with their parents and what power they have.

(Bavmorda interrupts her.)

Lord Bavmorda

Enough Blink! They are just kids; they don't know anything!

Blink

Oh great, then it will be easy to kill them.

Lord Bavmorda

Girls! Run!

Fiona

No, we want to stay and fight.

Clemence

Yes, this is our fight you told us.

Blink *(in an eerie voice)*

Oh, look! Surprisingly they are both willing to die.

Lord Bavmorda *(thinks for a few seconds before replying)*
Girls, I will handle her and you handle them.

(He points at more followers of Earl Zyrian, who are zombies wearing black robes.)

Blink
I think, Bavmorda, you forgot who I am and what I can do.

Lord Bavmorda
No, I have not, but I hope after killing Earl Zyrian, I will forget you too. Girls, run between the two hills and attack the army of Earl Zyrian.

(This time the girls make it and Blink is left near Bavmorda as she cannot go between the hills.)

Blink *(dropping her head to the left)*
You got my weak point.

Lord Bavmorda
I have known you for ages, Blink.

Chapter 12

Meeting Earl Zyrian

(Lord Bavmorda reaches near the girls by using Temarix, a teleporting spell.)

Blink to Bavmorda *(near the two hills)*

Are you hiding in there because you got scared of me? I know I can't come, but surely, someone else can, and I hope that you didn't forget him, Lord Bavmorda.

Fiona

Who is she, Bavmorda, and who is she talking about?!

Blink *(in a ghostly voice)*

Oh! Little girl, you will meet him very soon.

Lord Bavmorda *(with fear)*

No way! He can't be here.

Blink

Well! He is.

(Someone speaks in a spectral but loud voice from right behind Bavmorda.)

A man in a black mask

Hello Bavmorda! Forgot me?

Bavmorda

I can never forget you, Earl Zyrian.

Clemence

What? Earl Zyrian!

Bavmorda

Girls, put your defences up.

Earl Zyrian

Not this fast.

'Syldona'

(Clemence and Fiona dodge the attack, they start defending, shielding and firing. At a point, Fiona focuses all her energy to cast a powerful spell. She fires this spell at Earl Zyrian but he disappears in mid-air. He suddenly reappears behind them, grabs Clemence from the back and points his wand at her neck.

Bavmorda frees her by casting a spell that hits Earl Zyrian on his hand. The spell causes a huge gash on his hand. He moves back and casts a spell from which Bavmorda flies off and hits the castle where the girls have been sleeping. The girls are left with no option but to fight. Clemence casts a spell at him and he casts the antithetical of that spell. Then Fiona casts a spell and he hits the same spell back onto the girls. The girls look at each other. They both cast the same spell at the same time. He manages to cast the opposite of Fiona's spell but is unable to do so for Clemence's spell. He stands there frozen. The girls take this opportunity and run towards Bavmorda. Blink starts to follow by blinking her eyes. The girls start to fight Blink. Meanwhile, Cordelia appears. She sees the Portal open and closes it. Blink, Earl Zyrian, and their army disappear because the Portal is now off. Cordelia sees Bavmorda smashed in the castle. She goes to help him and sees the girls. She and the girls help Lord Bavmorda by casting healing spells.)

Chapter 13

The Never Forgotten Story of LOGSTON

(The girls ask Cordelia what has brought her here)

Cordelia

Girls, I came here to tell you a story and I saw you and Bavmorda fight the Glorious.

Clemence *(asking in confusion)*

What does that mean?

Cordelia

Earl Zyrian called his army the Glorious because he gathered some powerful and evil wizards and witches in his army.

Clemence

Oh, got it! And what story do you want to tell us?

Cordelia

About your parents. You always wanted to know it, and today I will tell you.

Fiona

Why this sudden decision?

Cordelia

Well, yesterday I talked to Lord Bavmorda using Hailet.

(The girls open their mouths to ask but Cordelia interrupts)

Cordelia

Before you ask, yes, you can talk using Hailet. When we were talking, Lord Bavmorda told me that you were very curious to know what had happened to your parents. That is when I decided that I would come over today and tell you about everything. However, when I told him about my visit, he disagreed. Yet, I really wanted to come today because I had a feeling that something would go wrong. So, I came and the rest you know. *(A slight pause.)* Do you want to hear the story about your parents now, or do you have more questions to ask?

Clemence and Fiona *(at the same time)*

Oh yes, tell us!

Cordelia *(smiling)*

Listen then. A long time ago Earl Zyrian broke into the Lizoria.

Fiona

Wait! What is Lizoria?

Cordelia

It's a library that contains *The Charten*. I hope Lord Bavmorda told you what *The Charten* means?

Clemence *(in an impatient voice)*

Yeah! We know what *The Charten* means and we also know how he became the Earl.

Cordelia

Okay then! So, after he became Earl, he started to destroy the Wizoleria and LOGSTON – Wizoleria is like a country in which LOGSTON is a city. Got it?

Clemence *(nodding her head)*

Please continue.

Cordelia

When he was destroying a part of Wizoleria, he killed many people including an old witch who used to live in LOGSTON. She was really old – at least 280 years! *(The girls try to interrupt but Cordelia understands their question and replies right away.)* Yes, witches and wizards can live for more than 100 years – their approximate age is 900 years. Also, if someone kills a witch or wizard who is more than 250 years old then the killer gets a curse. According to the curse, that person will live only for 200 years.

Earl Zyrian was around 50 years old when he got that curse. After he realised what he had done, he called an astrologer who told the Earl that he could live for more than 200 years if he wouldn't kill anyone hereafter.

Earl Zyrian thought to himself that he would quit killing. But he could not kill his desire to rule the world. After some time of not having killed people himself, he lost power. People stopped fearing him and to gain back his power he decided to kill all people that were against him. He also killed non-magical people to give threats that he could do anything.

(The girls ask whether non-magical people came to LOGSTON and Cordelia answers that they cannot.)

Cordelia *(continuing)*

He got so lost in his greed for power that he forgot what the astrologer had told him, and one night when he was destroying a part of LOGSTON, he saw the same astrologer. The astrologer told him that as he still hadn't given up death-dealing, he was giving him a curse for a lifetime. He further said that two girls from the royal bloodline would kill him and nobody would be able to stop them. They would make his dreadful reign come to an end and make this world as peaceful as it was earlier. Earl Zyrian got angry and killed the astrologer but since then he has been curious to know who are the two girls who might kill him. Thus, he called a witch named Blink.

Fiona

Oh! That is how Blink came into the picture!

Cordelia

Yeah! He asked Blink to find out about these two girls. Blink being the master of astrology, it was easy for her to find out. She told that the two girls were the daughters of Lady Glinda and Lord Abraham. Earl Zyrian got furious after hearing this. He could not bear that his mortal enemy and The Superior of Wizoleria had the power to kill him. He started searching for ways to meet you but he could not. At last, one day when both of you were visiting the main dome of the city with your parents, he attacked you but your parents protected you and gave me your responsibility. Your mother commanded me to leave LOGSTON. She was the only woman who had read *The Charten* till then. *(Sighing)* She was also my sister. Knowing that I had to protect you, I had to follow her commands. So, I left LOGSTON with both of you.

Clemence

What?! You were her sister?

Cordelia

Yeah!

Fiona

Aw!

Cordelia

Bavmorda stayed here to protect LOGSTON and he became The Superior. After a week, Bavmorda sent a letter to me and I was shocked to read that letter. The letter said that Glinda and Lord Abraham had died while fighting. I had known that Glinda would die but the death of Lord Abraham came as a shock.

(The girls do not react to that statement and so Cordelia continues to speak.)

Cordelia

The day when she gave me your responsibility, I heard her scream and I knew what had happened.

(She breaks into a sob and the girls comfort her.)

Cordelia *(after regaining her composure)*

I knew I had to take care of you. Then, somewhat after 15 years, Bavmorda sent a letter for the two of you and the rest you know.

Clemence

It's really great of you to tell us what had happened. It must have been very tough for you to talk about the past. I know there is a lot of pain that you carry within you. Thank you for telling us the story and also for taking care of us... *(pauses)* But I do have one more question – why do Earl Zyrian and Glorious live in that Portal?

Cordelia

After your mother died, Earl Zyrian killed Lord

Abraham. If one kills The Superior one faces repercussions. There is an old punishment that says:

Killing the Superior is a grand mistake
You will be locked in a chamber for
everyone's sake.

As the punishment states, the person will stay locked in the chamber till the Superior's own blood opens the chamber. Earl Zyrian made his army in that chamber and he can only come out of it when the two of you open the Portal. However, the Portal can be switched off by anyone of the royal bloodline.

Clemence

I know that our questions are unending but please, please tell me one more thing. Since our parents had both read *The Charten*, does it make them superior or something?

Cordelia

Yes, you both came from the generation of Superiors. Your grandfather was a superior too and one can only be a superior if he or she has read *The Charten*.

Fiona *(clearly stunned by all this)*

Oh my!

Clemence

But how did Lord Bavmorda know we were in the chasm?

Cordelia

He used your wands to track you.

Fiona

How do you know that?

Cordelia

That is what everyone does here.

Clemence

Oh!

Fiona

Just one more question.

Cordelia

Go on then.

Fiona

Why can't Blink go between the two hills?

Cordelia

Ah! It's because of an old curse she got! She used to be one of the most precise and smartest astrologers in the whole world but she kept using her knowledge in wrong things like helping Earl Zyrian. So, a superior bound her with old magic saying that she can't go in the most sacred places and the place between those two hills is quite sacred due to its rich history. Got it?

(The three of them chat for a while longer and then Cordelia says that they should get some rest and sleep for a while.)

Chapter 14

The Secret of the Stone

(Unable to sleep, the girls talk in their bed.)

Fiona

Time went by so fast.

Clemence

Yeah, I know.

Cordelia

Girls, what happened?

Fiona

Nothing. Just some bedtime talk.

Cordelia

Okay but sleep in a few minutes. You have to wake up early tomorrow.

Clemence

Okay. Good night!

(Cordelia turns off the lights and the girls go off to sleep soon after. They had a dream of their mother again.)

Glinda

Very good girls. Keep it up! However, there is one more thing you need to do. It is to kill Zyrian for good and I am going to give you one more hint about how you can kill him. I have requested Cordelia to take you to Blood Lake and you will find the stone which I have told you about earlier. The stone looks the same as the one that Cordelia has on her necklace. I gave Cordelia the necklace when she took you away from LOGSTON. Just combine both the stones and a new spell would be formed. It is called Unioft. That spell will empower you to kill Zyrian. It's the only way to kill him.

(The girls suddenly wake up. They talk about their dream and realise that yet again they both had the same dream.)

Chapter 15

Blood Lake and the Mysterious Signboard

Clemence

Come on, just take us!

Cordelia

Girls, that's way too dangerous...People had died in that lake. It is filled with blood!

Fiona

That's the interesting thing about it and we must go there. Cordelia, try to understand.

Cordelia

I still don't know why you have suddenly become so adamant about going to this lake. But I know that I will not be able to talk you out of it. So, get ready in five.

Fiona and Clemence together

YESS!

(The girls meet Cordelia in between the two hills after getting ready.)

Cordelia

Girls, I need to tell you something. It's more like a story. *(The girls nod and Cordelia continues.)* It's about how the blood lake became the Blood Lake. The story is quite a gory one. One day your grandmother went to visit a lake to meet an old friend. When she reached the lake, she saw Earl Zyrian. He was killing everyone there. She tried to protect the people but she was attacked by Earl Zyrian from the back. He bruised her right arm, her wand fell down, and he threw her into the lake. He threw many people into the lake that day. Due to this, eventually, the colour of the crystal-clear lake turned a bloody red. This is why it's called the Blood Lake. Your mother told me that there is a secret in the lake which is related to your grandmother.

Clemence

I think it is the stone that is linked to the necklace that you are wearing.

(She takes off the necklace and hands it to the girls.)

Fiona

Cordelia, we also have something to tell you. We... Uh... it's about mum and the stone you are talking about. I know it will be hard to believe but it is what it is. We get these strange dreams sometimes – both of us have the same dream – in which we can talk to mum. Last night, we had such a dream where mum told us that there was a stone in the Blood Lake which when combined with the stone of your necklace will make Unioft. She also said that once we make Unioft, it will help us to kill Zyrian.

Cordelia

Oh! It all makes sense now – your grandmother had the same stone as I have.

Clemence

Do you think that grandmother knew that with her stone she could destroy Earl Zyrian?

Cordelia

I think she knew, but I think Earl Zyrian also knew, and that is the reason why he killed your grandmother.

Fiona

You are right. Earl Zyrian must have known too.

Clemence

Shall we go to the Blood Lake now? We need to find the stone, remember?

Cordelia

Right! But before that, we need to get some Lalimeda.

Clemence

Now, what is that?

Cordelia

It's a plant that helps you breathe under the Blood Lake. We need to go to the G of LOGSTON to get that. Girls, hold my arm.

(The girls are confused but they do it anyway. Cordelia says 'tenlure' and the two girls feel as if they are being sucked. In a fraction of a second, they arrive in front of a tiny shop named Piante Acquatiche, meaning aquatic plants in Italian. They enter the shop and find that it is filled with little, big, mysterious and unique plants. Cordelia heads towards the counter

where she sees a woman who seems to be Italian.)

Fiona

Wow! But how did we reach here?

Cordelia

We simply teleported.

Clemence

You need to teach me how to do that.

Fiona

Me too…I really don't want to walk to the kitchen from my room anymore – it's really far away.

Cordelia *(with a tiny smile that soon disappears and her look becomes serious again)*
Not now. Right now, we need some Lalimeda first.

The Woman in the Shop

Ciao! Cosa ti porta qui? (Hello! What brings you here?)

Cordelia

Ciao. Ho bisogno di un po' Lalimeda (Hello. I need some Lalimeda.)

The Woman in the Shop

Sicuro. Aspetta un attimo, ce l'ho qui da qualche parte. (Sure. Wait a minute, I have it somewhere here.)
(The owner starts looking in the drawer next to the counter.)

The Woman in the Shop *(taking a sloppy green plant out)*
Trovato! Ecco qua, signorina! (Found it! There you go, young lady!)

Cordelia *(taking the plant)*
Grazie mille. (Thank you very much.)

Fiona
Which language was that?

Cordelia
Italian. The shopkeeper was an Italian; that's why. I learnt it when I was a child.

Clemence
What if someone doesn't know Italian? What will he/she do?

Cordelia

Most people have a translator in their wands.

Fiona

Oh!

Clemence

So, we have to hold your arm again to go to the Blood Lake?

Cordelia

Yes.

*(The girls hold Cordelia's arm. After a few seconds, at the O of LOGST***O***N, they arrive and see a red coloured lake and a signboard that says Blood Lake. The signboard has the same story written on it that Cordelia had told them. Fiona briefly reads the story and gets shocked to read the full names of Zyrian and Bavmorda. Both Cordelia and Clemence think Fiona's reaction is because of the scary blood in the lake. But something else seems to have struck Fiona. Fiona stands still in complete silence and then shakes her head to bring her back in the present moment and to continue the quest to find the stone and to look for some answers.)*

Chapter 16

The Undine

Cordelia

It's time to have Lalimeda.

(She hands some of the leaves of the plant to each of them. The girls and Cordelia eat the leaves.)

Fiona

Eww! It tastes awful.

Cordelia *(wiping her mouth with a handkerchief)*

Well, this is the only way to survive under the Blood Lake. Let's go girls.

(Cordelia leads and the girls follow until Cordelia comes to a complete stop. She tells the girls to dive with her and swim to the shore and the girls do as she instructs. After a few minutes, the girls and Cordelia feel the surface beneath them so they stand straight. It is pitch dark down here. Cordelia takes out her wand and casts a spell creating a ball that is giving out light. The girls copy Cordelia and originate their own light balls. They start to look around until Fiona feels very

cold. Cordelia says it's just the water. After looking around for a while Clemence sees a giant mansion near a bunch of dead bodies. She hints to Cordelia and Fiona that she has found something. As soon as she goes near the bodies, she feels extreme cold – as if she is in Antarctica. Fiona and Cordelia also feel the same. Fiona suggests going back but Cordelia insists that they carry on. Clemence agrees with Cordelia and continues to walk. Clemence suddenly stops dead in her tracks. She feels as if there is a hand on her shoulder; the hand is as cold as death. She screams at top of her voice and draws the attention of Fiona and Cordelia who are trying to find a way to get over the dead bodies. Clemence looks over her shoulder and sees a face as blue as the sky – a ghostly female figure. As Clemence looks down, she observes that the ghost is floating an inch above the ground. The ghost looks as though she is made of deep blue water! By the time Clemence realises it is a ghost, Cordelia casts a spell that causes a beam of periwinkle light to erupt from her wand. The ghost that has been standing in front of Clemence glides off in the opposite direction. Clemence is too shocked to move. Fiona makes her way to Clemence and says, 'We should go before that ghost comes again'. Cordelia runs towards both girls and says, 'Girls let's go in and get that stone'. Fiona and Cordelia argue about whether or not to get the stone.

Meanwhile, Clemence stands there and watches them, too stunned to say anything after seeing the ghost. Cordelia and Fiona's argument seems never-ending. So Clemence shouts, 'WE ARE GOING IN AND GETTING THAT STONE, I AM IN NO MOOD OF COMING DOWN HERE AGAIN'. After this, she starts to make her way over the bodies. Cordelia says, 'Clemence come back here – there must be danger there. You don't know, there might be another Undine there'. Clemence ignores this and makes her way to the mansion. As soon as she touches the handle of the door to open it, the light balls that have been giving them the light start to flicker. Clemence feels someone's presence other than Cordelia and Fiona. Before she knows what is happening, she is smashed in rock and she sees the same ghost. The ghost's hair is flying in every direction and her eyes turn from extreme white to green. A yellow light ball is in her hand.

Clemence tries to get up but can't – the ghost starts to make her way towards her. Clemence panics and turns so that she lies on her stomach. She starts to climb up the rock. She sees Cordelia and Fiona from the corner of her eye. They try to move but are unable to. As Clemence tries to climb up the rock, she feels really sharp nails digging into her feet. Her feet are now extremely cold. She realises that the ghost is dragging her into that mansion. Soon after she finds herself in total darkness. She hears Cordelia and Fiona screaming; they are both calling her name. She feels cold and her feet feel sore but it still has the presence of someone's hand on them. Her voice is tired from shouting while the ghost had been dragging her. She feels herself drifting away and then she faints.)

Chapter 17

Undine – The Guardian of the Stone

(Cordelia and Fiona return home after seeing what happened to Clemence. They both think she is dead. Fiona cries all the way home for the loss of her sister. Cordelia tells her to calm down. She says that they will find a way to get Clemence back.)

Fiona *(crying)*

How do you expect me to calm down? We have no clue where Clemence is or how she is. I don't even know if she is alive or not.

Cordelia

I know you are worried but you can't panic or cry. We need to find a way to get her back. We can't just go down there. Undines are dangerous. We need to bring Clemence back before something happens to her, and we will.

Fiona *(sobbing)*

What are we supposed to do if we can't go down there? Clemence is in danger! What shall we do now?

Cordelia

We can go to Lord Bavmorda to seek help. But he would not be able to accompany us or help us a lot.

Fiona

Why can't he help us?

Cordelia

Bavmorda gave half his power to you and Clemence to empower you both. If he goes to the Blood Lake, he will lose the other half too.

Fiona *(her sobbing lesser now but looking quite upset)*

You might have a point. Let's go to Lord Bavmorda.

(They both head to Lord Bavmorda's room in the castle.)

Cordelia *(sitting near Bavmorda)*

Hey, how are you feeling?

Bavmorda *(giving a small smile)*

I have been better. But it was important to empower the young girls.

Fiona *(sadness in her voice)*

We need to ask you something, Lord Bavmorda.

(Bavmorda looks at Fiona, and then at Cordelia. He stays silent for a while and then asks.)

Lord Bavmorda

What is going on?

(Cordelia tells Bavmorda everything about the ghost and Clemence.)

Lord Bavmorda

I think your suspicions are correct – it is an Undine. It will be difficult to get Clemence back but there is good news, Fiona. I don't think Clemence is dead because only on very rare occasions do Undines kill.

Fiona

What is an Undine? And what does she want from Clemence?

Bavmorda

Undine is a female spirit who inhabits the water. She protects old sacred magic and, from what I think, she was protecting the stone. An Undine has no intention to kill though.

Fiona

Do you think we can go into the lake and talk to her?

Bavmorda

It will be difficult but I know you are more powerful than any challenge that comes your way.

Cordelia

Do you think it will be safe, Bavmorda?

Bavmorda *(casting a protective spell 'Tigen' on them)*
I can't guarantee Cordelia but you must try.

(Cordelia and Fiona thank Bavmorda, take some Lalimeda from the castle and head towards the Blood Lake. They both dive in and go towards the mansion they had seen earlier.)

Fiona

Hello? Anyone here? Clemence?

(They both hear some crackling behind them and turning around they see the Undine. She does not look angry. She appears to be quite calm.)

The Undine *(in a sweet melodic voice)*

What do you want? Why are you here?

Fiona

When we came here the last time, we were three. My sister was trying to get into the mansion but you took her away. The mansion has a stone and we need to find that stone to kill Earl Zyrian.

The Undine *(a bit of anger in her voice but a melodic tune)*

You think I am going to believe you? There was a boy before you three and he had lied.

Cordelia

Please believe us. We have no reason to lie to you.

The Undine *(no anger in her voice)*

The stone is sacred. It was Lydia Laveau's stone and only her blood can take it.

Fiona

I know her! She is my grandmother; I am Fiona Laveau. And the other girl who came with us last time, is my sister, Clemence Laveau.

The Undine *(a bit surprised)*

Indeed, the name matches my list of the bloodline. You both need to wait here; I will bring the stone and your sister here.

(The Undine turns and starts gliding towards the mansion. After a few minutes, Clemence comes out of the mansion, following The Undine.)

The Undine *(handing the cyan-coloured bright stone to Fiona)*

Here you are.

'Hope you see the shadow in the Chasm'

(Fiona takes the stone and as she holds the stone it started to emit a bright blue light. The three of them thank The Undine. They start making their way up to the top of the lake. All three of them come out and teleport to the castle. Both the girls are able to cast their spells now. Clemence tells Fiona about how she had

fainted and then had woken up just a few minutes ago to see The Undine. After that, she followed her to Cordelia and Fiona. Cordelia tells them that she had fainted because of the magic of The Undine.)

Chapter 18

The Last Fight

Clemence *(back in the castle)*
Guys, ready to merge the stones?

Cordelia *(hands the stone from her necklace)*
Yes! Girls, here you go – my stone.

Fiona *(keeping the stone on the table along with Cordelia's stone)*
And here is grandma's stone.

(The two stones merge and make a bright amber coloured stone, as bright as the Sun.)

Fiona
We did it!

Cordelia
Yes. But do you guys have any idea how to use it?

Clemence *(shakes her head from side to side)*
No.

Cordelia

Absolutely no idea?

Fiona

Nope.

Cordelia

Well, then we need to start finding out.

Fiona

How about we ask Bavmorda?

Clemence

I don't think he will know, but we can try.

Cordelia

Right! Let's ask him.

(They all head to Bavmorda's room.)

Fiona

Bavmorda, we need your help again. We don't know how to use Unioft.

Lord Bavmorda *(smilingly)*

You have been empowered girls. You would know that intuitively.

Clemence

What? How?

Cordelia

Okay then! Let's go girls. Bavmorda has guided you.

(All three of them exit.)

Fiona *(recalling what she read on the signboard)*

I have a question, Cordelia.

Cordelia

Go ahead, ask.

Fiona

Why do we need to kill Earl Zyrian? I mean why can't he just stay in that chamber?

Cordelia

You both need to kill him because after some time the chamber will break and he will be out again.

Usually, chambers like these don't break easily but Earl Zyrian and his glorious army is too powerful to stay in that chamber. That's why you need to finish him for good.

Fiona

Oh! I get it now. But I understand he comes from a very powerful family line. Would it be possible for us to kill him?

Cordelia

Yes, he comes from a very powerful family line but so do you!

(Fiona keeps on recalling the line on the signboard at the Blood Lake.)

Now come on let's create Unioft.

(The girls have an intuition about how to create Unioft. Fiona keeps her wand on top of Clemence's wand forming a cross. Then they put the stone at the centre of the cross. The stone shines bright, emitting powerful rays reaching the sky. The wands get empowered by the magnificent rays being emitted from the stone, and now the only thing left is to finish Earl Zyrian. Cordelia takes them to the chasm and tells them to open

the Portal. The girls do as they are told. All three of them start to look at the point from where Earl Zyrian should come out, but they can't see him anywhere. After a while, Fiona sees some shadows towards the end of the chasm. She quietly signals Cordelia and Clemence that she might have found him. Fiona walks quietly, trying her best not to make any noise. After a while, she hears a scream from Clemence. She turns and sees Cordelia fighting with the Glorious. She starts looking for Clemence and sees her fighting with Blink. Clemence is badly wounded. Fiona wants to go help her, but what shocks Fiona the most is that Earl Zyrian is nowhere to be seen. She hears footsteps behind her. She turns around and sees that Earl Zyrian is right behind her.)

Earl Zyrian

Nice to meet you again, Fiona.

Fiona *(with courage)*

Zyrian, it's over. You can't do anything.

Earl Zyrian

You think that after living in that chamber for years I will just let you win?

(Fiona is about to cast her spell but Earl Zyrian is faster and powerful. He casts a spell that hits Fiona in her left knee. She falls to the ground. Earl Zyrian points his wand at her neck.)

Fiona

You won't be able to succeed in it, Zyrian! I am telling you this.

Earl Zyrian

Oh! The little girl is as brave as her mum. Do you know your mum told me the same thing seconds before I killed her? *(He laughs an evil laughter.)*

Fiona

You may have the guts to kill me and haunt me in my dreams. But you will never have the guts to accept the mistakes you made. Why did you kill your sister?

(Zyrian takes a step back and opens his mouth to say something. Meanwhile, Fiona tries to cast a few complex and powerful spells, but Zyrian is too powerful to even be touched by them. Zyrian casts the 'Syldona' spell to kill Fiona. She bends down to protect herself from the spell and accidently stumbles and falls backwards. The spell misses her by a fraction of a

millimetre. As she tries to regain her balance back, her attention goes to the shadow of Earl Zyrian in the chasm. She has a quick flashback of the Undine's words. She screams "Clemence, cast Unioft!" Clemence teleports herself in a fraction of second to Fiona and they cast Unioft's spell together at the shadow of Earl Zyrian in the chasm. Both spells hit Earl Zyrian's shadow at the same time and he dissolves to death. Clemence and Fiona help Cordelia after defeating Earl Zyrian. Cordelia heals Clemence's wounds and the girls help Cordelia heal her wounds by casting healing spells.)

Chapter 19

The Family Secret

Fiona

Clemence, how did you defeat Blink? I mean I didn't see her body anywhere near the other Glorious.

Clemence

She wounded me because she was way faster than I was. The only thing that I could think of then, to defeat her, was to freeze her eyes so that she could not blink anymore! Right after I froze her eyes she vanished. I asked Cordelia why that happened and Cordelia said that years ago Blink had received the gift of her special eyes from a superior. The superior had told her that as soon as her eyes would perish, she would perish too.

Fiona *(chuckling)*

Wow! You are really smart.

Clemence

Now you tell me, Fiona. What was the mistake that Earl Zyrian made?

Fiona

Do you know that Bavmorda is our father's brother?

Clemence

What?!

Fiona

Yes, and Zyrian is our mother's brother.

Clemence

Okay, now you are going crazy! And what is the justification that Bavmorda is our father's brother and *(hesitatingly)* Zyrian is our mother's brother?

Fiona

Remember when Cordelia told us that we came from a family of superiors? So, if our father was The Superior, and he is older than Bavmorda, what are the odds that Bavmorda stayed here and became The Superior? Moreover, how does he know so much about our grandmother, the stone and Unioft? And he also has the same surname as us. I read it on the signboard at the Blood Lake.

Clemence

Hmm, but even if Bavmorda is our uncle, how is Zyrian our mother's brother?

Fiona

Our mother's maiden surname is Wier. I know it's shocking but I read the signboard at the Blood Lake, remember?

Clemence

Yes, you were quite shocked after reading that but what has the signboard got to do with Zyrian being our uncle?

Fiona

The signboard read the full name of Zyrian; it is – Earl Zyrian Wier!

(Clemence takes in the information that she has just been given and asks.)

Clemence

Why didn't you speak up then?

Fiona

I wasn't sure earlier, but now I am, as our mother

was allowed to read *The Charten* being superior's wife. He must have been jealous so he broke the rules of LOGSTON and read *The Charten* without the permission of our dad, The Superior, which earned him a curse of short life and that was his mistake. You get it...does the story match?

Clemence

You are right, but why would he kill his own sister?

Fiona

He knew that the power of Unioft could kill him. As it was known only to his sister, so he killed her.

Clemence

That's sad. But our brave mother still managed to save her LOGSTON. So now what?

Fiona

Let's thank our aunt Cordelia and Uncle Bavmorda.

(The girls go to meet Uncle Bavmorda and Aunt Cordelia. They thank them. Girls look one more time around the place that had been a secret to them for almost 14 years, a place they loved. The girls and

Cordelia head back to their house.)

(Back to the house)

...

Fiona

The superheroes who saved the world need a vacation at the beach.

Clemence

And this time I agree with you. And you know what, we don't need to travel to the beach. We can teleport!

(The girls bicker for a while and then go to sleep peacefully.)